*For Harry, L.G.*
*For Nicholas and Ned, S.G.*

First published in Great Britain in 2008
by Piccadilly Press Ltd,
5 Castle Road, London NW1 8PR
www.piccadillypress.co.uk

Designed by Simon Davis
Printed and bound by WKT in China
Colour reproduction by Dot Gradations


ISBN: 978 1 85340 958 5 (hardback)
ISBN: 978 1 85340 957 8 (paperback)

1 3 5 7 9 10 8 6 4 2

A catalogue record of this book is available from the British Library

# The Best Jumper

Lynne Garner • Sarah Gill

Piccadilly Press • London

It was Spindle's birthday. He was very excited as he opened his presents. Finally, there was only one present left.

Spindle ripped off the paper
to find a mass of colours.
It was a jumper - the
BEST jumper he had
ever seen!

"Thank you,
Grandma,"
he said, putting it on.
"It fits perfectly."

After breakfast, Spindle
and his brother and sister
sailed his new boat on the pond.

Spindle's warm, snuggly
jumper kept out the chill.

Spindle LOVED wearing his jumper.

He wore it ALL the time.

And even when it was too hot to wear, he always took it with him . . . just in case.

One windy day, Spindle
decided to fly his kite.
The kite danced up and down, round and round,
just like a leaf.

Suddenly a huge gust of wind blew it high up into the trees, where it STUCK.

Spindle clambered up the
branches. But as he stretched
out his arm to free the kite . . .

he tore his
jumper!

RIP!
RIP!

Spindle ran indoors.
"Mama, there's a hole
in my best jumper!"
he cried.

"Don't worry, dear,"
Mama said, as she fetched
her sewing box.

Mama often insisted on washing Spindle's jumper.

It always smelled a bit
funny the next day.
But it soon got
back to normal.

As time went by,
Spindle found he had
to pull REALLY hard to get
his jumper on.

Then one day Spindle found even
when he pulled REALLY, REALLY hard,
it wouldn't go over his ears.

"My jumper's shrunk," he told Mama.
"No, it's you who are growing, dear,"
said Mama and she made two little slits in
the neck so it would fit again.

One night, when Spindle was staying
at Grandma's house, there was a big storm.
The thunder crashed and the lightning flashed.
Poor Spindle was very scared but he
didn't want to wake Grandma,
so he cuddled his jumper instead.

In the morning, Spindle's grandma said,
"Spindle, dear, that jumper's too small for you."

"No it's not," said Spindle,
trying to pull it over his tummy.

But he let Grandma
add some material
to the bottom and
the cuffs.

When Grandma next came to visit,
she brought Spindle a big parcel.

IT WAS
ANOTHER
JUMPER!

When Spindle put it on,
he found that the sleeves
were a little too long,

the neck was
a little too big,

and the waist was
a little too large.

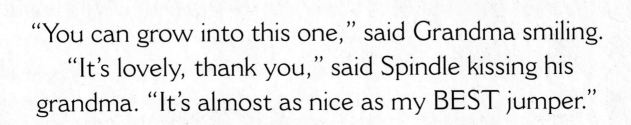

"You can grow into this one," said Grandma smiling.
"It's lovely, thank you," said Spindle kissing his
grandma. "It's almost as nice as my BEST jumper."

When Spindle went out to play,
he wore his new jumper.
But he took his BEST jumper with
him . . . just in case.

That evening, when Spindle was asleep,
Grandma was very busy with his old jumper . . .

The next day Grandma had another surprise for Spindle.
She held up a brightly coloured toy.
It was a RABBIT!
"I made it from your old jumper,"
she told him.

"Thank you," said Spindle.
"It's the BEST rabbit
in the world!"

And he took it with him
EVERYWHERE!